K

TWO TOO MANY

Written and Illustrated by Nora S. Unwin

The two little black kittens were lost in the forest and didn't understand that they were abandoned because they were "Two too many." They thought they were named "Two" and "Too Many." They found a little house and a huge black cat let them come in. There were strange preparations going on — the kittens didn't know it was Hallowe'en. They saw bats and spiders and a strange old woman who talked about flying potions for the broom. While the witch was chanting "Beegy, weegy, gora gallumph," she and the big black cat with the two little kittens hidden in the straw of the broom flew off to the Grand Moon Race. What a wild night for two little kittens! Did you see them flying through the air Hallowe'en night?

Classification and Dewey Decimal: Fiction (Fic)

About the Author and Illustrator:

NORA S. UNWIN came to the United States from England intending to stay only one year but has lived here ever since. She studied at the Royal College of Art in London. Her father was connected with publishing and she grew up surrounded by books. Miss Unwin makes her home in Wellesley, Massachusetts, where in addition to her writing, illustrating and print-making, she also teaches children's art classes in a private school.

TWO TOO ↑ MANY

Story and pictures by NORA S. UNWIN

1968 FIRST CADMUS EDITION
THIS SPECIAL EDITION IS PUBLISHED BY ARRANGEMENT WITH
THE PUBLISHERS OF THE REGULAR EDITION
DAVID MCKAY COMPANY, INC.
BY
E. M. HALE AND COMPANY
EAU CLAIRE, WISCONSIN

TWO TOO MANY

It was dark, pitch black, and two kittens were wandering in the woods. Treetops swished and creaked. Dry leaves muttered. Queer noises scared them. Lost and abandoned, they plodded on through the darkness with their ears laid back and their whiskers alert.

"Wish Mother were here to bring us a nice juicy mouse!"

"Or the Boss to give us a saucer of milk."
"Why did he say, 'You're Two Too Many'?"
" 'Cause that's what he called us, stupid."
"You mean—our real names?"
"Suppose so."
"Sounds queer to me."
They struggled on in silence for awhile.

"Which am I then?"

"You're Two. I'm Too Many, 'cause my tail is longer."

"How so?"

"Longer tail, longer name."

There was another silence while Two thought about his tail.

"I think mine's fatter," he said.

"But mine's longer."

"Mine's fatter."

"Longer."

"Fatter."

"Psst!"

They stopped talking.
"Look, I see something!"
"Where?"
"There."
"Is it a star?"
"Whatever it is, let's try to reach it."
As they pushed on, the tiny light grew stronger.
It seemed to come from a window and the window
belonged to a house. The house was very small and
crooked, but it had a door and a chimney.

7

The kittens hesitated, then they climbed the one rickety step and Too Many scratched gently at the door.

They heard a soft thud inside and the sound of paddy feet crossing the floor. They waited but nothing happened.

Two cocked his head to listen more closely.

"Somebody's snoring," he whispered.

Too Many scratched again at the door.

A low miaow sounded under the crack. "Who are you? What do you want?"

"We're lost and we're hungry."

"And we're tired of scrambling through the woods. May we come in?"

There was no answer, but the tip of one long whisker showed under the door.

"Who is we?" asked the cat voice.

"Two—Too Many," answered the kittens together.

"Heebly, weebly! What color are you?"

"Black."

"*All* black."

There was another long silence.

"We–ell, ll–ll, in that case maybe I can let you in, but not for long. It's nearly Hallowe'en, you know."

"Hello—who?" began Two, but at that moment there was a rattling of the latch. The door opened a crack, and there stood the biggest cat the kittens had ever seen. He was coal black, with enormous whiskers, and eyes of burning amber. The kittens quailed under his gaze, but the smell of warmth indoors was inviting.

"Follow me," said the big cat, motioning them in with a wave of his handsome tail.

They squeezed noiselessly through the opening
and looked about. The room was lighted by one
candle, and a little fire glowed on the hearth.
There wasn't much furniture, just a table, a chair,
an old chest, and a great high bed. In the bed was
a huge bumpy lump. This was where the snores
were coming from.

"What's that?" Too Many stood on his hind legs
to look.

12

"Better bat your blinkers, you'll soon see," whispered the big cat, "and then you'd best keep out of sight, because you *are* two too many, you know. Get dried off now and I'll see what I can spare for supper."

Without a sound, he opened a little trap door in the floor and disappeared. The kittens stared after him, but he didn't return.

"Better wash now."
"Gracious yes! You look awful."
"So do you."
"Not as bad as you."
"You do, too."
"Don't."
"Do."
"D—psst! What's that?"

They looked up. There was a brief commotion over their heads. Now the kittens saw dozens of rows of bats hanging from the rafters. The flickering candle cast great shadows about the room. It showed cobwebs which festooned the walls. It revealed a tall black hat hanging on a peg.

They also noticed a big besom leaning against the wall. Two black leather shoes lay side by side under the bed, the firelight reflected on their silver buckles. On a shelf by the candle a clock ticked steadily. Still the snoring went on, deep and even.

14

Suddenly the trap door opened noiselessly and the big cat reappeared. His mouth looked full and from it dangled two mouse tails. He laid his catch on the hearth. The kittens sniffed hopefully. They knew better than to pounce. The cat gave them a warning glance before he stretched up to a high shelf, poured something from a jug, and put a full saucer on the floor next to the mice.

"All yours," he said majestically, "but leave me the tails." He turned away and busied himself with a saucepan on the fire.

Two and Too Many each grabbed a mouse and ate ravenously. Two almost crunched the tail before Too Many stopped him. "Watch out, greedy! That's his, remember."

They drank every drop in the saucer. It wasn't at all like milk which they had been used to, but it tasted good.

They looked at each other. "Better wash now, like Mother said."

They started on a thorough cleaning, pink tongues busy, claws going to work. They bit out the burrs that had stuck to their coats in the woods and helped each other do behind the ears.

After scooping up the two mousetails and popping them in a cupboard, the big cat settled on the bedrail. The clock ticked on, the snoring continued, and the amber eyes watched.

The kittens had reached their tails and were just about to wash the last inch when suddenly from the candle shelf there came a deafening racket. *Burrrr-rrrrr-rr-r-r-r-r-r-r-r!!!!* All bedlam seemed let loose at once.

Two and Too Many shot straight up in the air and down again, their fur standing out like porcupine quills. All the bats left their moorings and went whirling around the room. The spiders throbbed on their webs. The broom in the corner fell down with a clatter. The big cat leaped from the bedrail and landed on the bump in the bed. He clawed back the coverlet with a shrill "Mia–o–oww!" Swiftly he pounced at the clock, knocking it to the floor. There it whirred to a stop.

In their fright the kittens rushed for safety and hid behind the great bushy broom where they crouched, trembling. Soon they realized the room was quiet again. The snoring had stopped. They peered out from their hiding place.

Gradually the hump in the bed rolled over and two long skinny hands appeared. They had knobby knuckles and yellow fingernails. Slowly the hump rose up, and there sat the ugliest old woman the kittens had ever seen. She had a big hook nose, a chin like a hatchet, straggly white hair, and eyes as yellow as the big cat's. When she gave an enormous yawn, her teeth looked like bits of coal.

She glared about her, frowning. "Grizzle my gizzard, another year gone by?" She scratched her head, rubbed her eyes, and stared at the big cat on the bedrail. "Blackington, what have you got for me to eat?"

With one flying jump, the big cat left the bedrail and disappeared into the cupboard. Before you could say "Snice mice twice" he was back, carrying a platter between two paws which he placed before her. On it were seven skinned frogs lying on a dock leaf, with a large pile of stewed mousetails heaped beside this, like pink spaghetti.

"Is this all you've got?" snapped the old witch, gobbling up the delicacies easily. "No finger-toe broth or pickled ears?"

She looked fierce, but the big cat did not appear in the least afraid of her. He bounced to the cupboard once more and brought out a tall brown jar. The witch sniffed at it, then gulped down its contents, looking quite pleased.

"That's better, that's better," she said. "Now, I must get dressed. Is the flying potion ready?"

Blackington ran to the saucepan and stirred it vigorously. Little poppings and bubblings could be heard. The kittens glanced at each other and shivered. "Maybe we should get out of here quick, before *we* get put into that pot," whispered Two.

"But how can we?" Too Many whispered back.

At that moment, the old witch clambered out of bed and stomped over to the chest. She opened it with a bang, drew out an assortment of garments, and proceeded to dress herself.

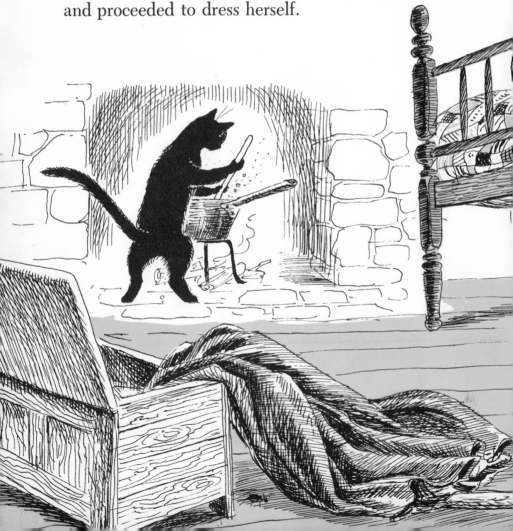

First, she pulled on some long black stockings and fastened a striped yellow petticoat over her nightie. Next, she put on a black checked petticoat, then a black one with yellow spots, and lastly an old black skirt. Over this went a tight black bodice, hooked with hawks' claws down the front. She screwed her hair back and fastened it with a goose's wishbone, tied a white cap on under her chin. Finally she lifted the tall black hat from its peg and jammed it firmly on her head.

"Blackington, where are my shoes?" she demanded.

In a trice, Blackington had them out from under the bed and helped her slip them on, but one was short its button.

"Drat those rats," scolded the witch, "they must have gnawed it off. Have you been off guard, Blackington?" The big cat disappeared, but returned in a moment with some string to tie on the shoe.

While this was going on, a large spider suddenly dropped on its web and hung right in front of Too Many's nose, making him cross-eyed.

"Better get out of this," it whispered, "if you don't want a ride."

The kittens were too startled to answer. The spider climbed back to the beam. Before Two and Too Many could look for escape, more things began to happen.

"Now," cried the witch, fastening on a large black cloak, "it's time we were off or we'll be late. I'd like to win the trophy this year. Is the potion strong? Put plenty of it on my broom and give me the soaring dust to go in my pocket. We're sure to need it for the Grand Moon Race."

As she spoke, she bent down and grasped the broom handle and set it upright. The kittens noticed a twinkle in her eye that they could not see before. They dared not run, so they clung fast to the bristles. The light in the room was dim and they were so black that they were practically invisible.

Blackington was so busy that he had quite forgotten them.

While the witch was watching the big cat, the kittens crept further and further in between the bristles of the besom.

Blackington brought the pot from the fire and before you could say "Spider inside her," the powerful flying potion was being sprinkled over the witch, the broom, the big cat, and all. Now the witch began to chant hoarsely:

"*Beegy, weegy, gora gallump,*
Crankity, cronkity, grambley gump,
Heebaly, hobbaly, jambly jomp,
Katchaby, koobaly, langery nomp."

While she chanted she circled slowly, turning the broom as she went. The spiders throbbed in their webs till they glittered like stars in the candlelight. The bats came down from the rafters, circling and twittering. The witch's voice grew louder. Now it was shrill:

"*Skeelagy, weelagy, oobigy skee,*
Quilam–n, plyam–n, hilergy, spreeeeeee."

At the last line she almost shrieked. She waved
her cloak and straddled the broom. The door flew
open and Blackington leaped to the handle, his
claws dug well in. With a rushing sound of wind,

the broom rose from the floor and shot through
the open door amidst a cloud of bats and a shower
of dust. Up, up it went, weaving through spaces in
the trees till it gained the open sky.

Down in the cottage, the candle had blown out.
The clock still ticked, but only the spiders were
there to hear it.

From their precarious perch inside the broom, the kittens couldn't see a thing. That was because their eyes were tight shut. Their ears were laid flat and their claws dug in for dear life. But they could feel the rushing of wind, and each knew the other was there.

"Where are we? What's happened?" Two managed to whisper.

"Goodness knows! But I guess this is what the spider meant," Too Many replied.

"Yes, I remember now, a ride. Who would have thought it meant this! Shall we ever come back?"

"Where are we going? That's what I'd like to know."

Too Many dared to open his eyes and glanced downward. "Look," he said, "look at all those lights! They can't be stars either." He slithered down the broom a bit to get a better look.

Two ventured to change his position.

To their surprise they heard the witch call out, "Blackington, we're not well balanced tonight. Something is different. Have you been sharpening your claws on my broom again and breaking some of the bristles?"

The big cat swished his tail and said nothing.

The escorting bats circled the riders constantly.

"I distinctly felt a tail-wobble, and it isn't the wind," the witch went on.

The kittens dared not move.

"Ah," she said presently, "maybe my cloak is caught." The witch made a quick movement and the broom dipped suddenly. The kittens were unprepared.

Too Many lost his grip and slithered perilously near the end of the bristles, clutching madly with his outspread claws and trying to find a fresh grip. He was hanging now only by two feet, but he clung on.

Very cautiously Two slid himself backward, tail
extended, hoping to give his brother aid. Just as
the tip of his tail was within Too Many's reach, the
wind caught the witch's cloak. The end of it
flapped wildly behind her and slapped against the
broom. It almost enveloped the kittens before it
tugged away again. They lost their hold. Next
minute they were falling one behind the other,
down—down—down—down toward the lights
below.

Strangely enough, they did not fall fast. Some of the flying potion had got sprinkled on them, too, but once they let go of the broom it had less effect. However, they were sailing quite gently. After turning several somersaults, they spread their tails and toes to act as parachutes, and landed safely on their feet.

Two landed last, because his tail was fattest.

He biffed Too Many on the head. They both felt
dazed. "What happened? Where are we?"

They tried to walk, but their legs were wobbly.
"I'm sort of sorry to miss that ride. Wonder where
they are off to?"

"I wonder where *we* are," remarked Two, giving
himself a good shake and trying his legs again on
the grassy lawn.

Too Many peered about him. Suddenly he shot
fifteen inches into the air, landing stiffly on all
fours, every hair bristling. He spat loudly.

"Whatever's the matter?" gasped Two. He
turned around and was *he* surprised!

There, just a few feet away, was an en
face staring at them. A great orange face with no
body, no arms or legs, it was sitting on the ground
and laughing at them.

"Twist my tail! What's so funny?" called Too
Many to the face when he had recovered from his
fright. "You wouldn't think it was so funny if you'd
just fallen miles through the air."

He stalked stiffly up to the great face. Still it
grinned. The eyes flickered wickedly. Too Many
backed away. Two peered closer. "Is it alive?"

"Don't know, it smells warm."

"Dare you to pat it."

"I'd rather pounce on it."

"No, pat it."

"No, pounce on it."

"Pat it!"

"Pounce on it!"

"Pat—"

"Psst! Somebody's coming, hide!"

Together the kittens raced for safety through some shrubs. But there, on the other side, on a doorstep, sat another great orange face, glaring down at them.

"Singe my whiskers! That one looks fierce."

They darted across a driveway. There was yet another face, with even bigger teeth than the one before. On they went, scrambling through bushes, under fences, even crossing a street, fearing they heard footsteps behind them.

Everywhere they went, orange faces seemed to peer at them—grinning, solemn, smiling, surprised, big-mouthed, cross-eyed, large, small, high, low, wide or shiny. Many of the faces seemed to have bright lights coming from inside them which made them more scary than ever.

"Come on, let's climb a tree and get away from them!" called Too Many.

He darted under some low boughs and started up a spruce. Two followed him. Soon they were lost in the thick evergreen branches. But before they reached the top, they felt the tree shudder. Something had landed in it.

The kittens peered. The object dangling from a branch was long and black. Something on it shone like silver. Too Many crawled near to it to have a closer look.

"Why, it's the old witch's shoe!" he called to Two. "The one that was tied on! Come and help me untangle the string."

While they were working at it there was a sudden rush of wind over their heads and a cloud of bats flew by.

"Creeping claws! That means the witch herself isn't far off."

They flattened themselves on the branch and shut their eyes. In a moment they could hear the witch's croaky voice calling:

> *"Shoe, shoe, show yourself, do!*
> *Drat that lost button,*
> *Who'll find me my shoe?"*

Without stopping to think, the kittens mewed, "Here! Here! We've found your shoe."

It was Blackington who heard them. Immediately he steered the broom low toward the tree. The kittens saw his great yellow eyes shining like lamps.

"Look out!" cried the witch. "Wherever are you going? We'll smash into that tree if you're not careful." She shook out an ample amount of soaring powder to save herself, as she thought, from disaster.

It did the trick. It landed on the shoe which slowly began to rise in the air.

The dust landed on the kittens too. With their claws still tangled in the string they also rose into the air.

"Scroopy scrimpings! Never thought I'd see you two again," miaowed Blackington as he reached out a paw to catch the shoe. "You've done us a good turn and no mistake. Saved the night, in fact. Jump on behind, we may need you again."

"Dare you?" whispered Two to Too Many, but there was no time to argue about it. Almost before they knew what was happening, the kittens found themselves enveloped in the witch's cloak again. The broom was skimming the rooftops and the witch was as pleased as a pumpkin to have her shoe back again.

"At least this is better than meeting all those faces," whispered Two.

"And maybe it will be fun after all," replied Too Many, feeling braver this time.

And fun it certainly was!

Now the witch was in a jovial mood. She went roof-hopping all over the town. She puffed down chimneys, she beat a tattoo with her heels on the shingles. She stopped electric clocks and set all the church bells ringing. She sent down the bats to bother the street lamps and scare the people. She shook the last apples off the trees, tipped over pumpkins, blew out candles, whistled through key holes, and set all the dogs to barking and the cats to caterwauling.

The kittens thought it hilarious!

"My, what a rough night!" the old folks said as they peered nervously out doors, while the children went shrieking and laughing through the streets.

The old clock in the church tower struck eleven booming strokes.

"Gracious gruncious," said the witch, "it's time to go or we'll never get into the Grand Race."

Blackington knew what this meant. He sent a message to the kittens by a spider who rode in a crack of the broom handle. "Tell those two behind to hang on tight, we'll be going top speed."

The spider crawled down the handle to where the kittens crouched, their backs to the witch. He delivered the message.

"But where are we going?" asked Too Many.

"It's the *Grand Race* over the moon."

"The moon?"

"Happens every Hallowe'en when the moon is up."

"Kippery, flippery, sounds exciting!"

"It is, but be sure you hold tight now and keep your eyes open." The spider crawled back into his crack.

Already the broom was mounting, gathering speed.

The moon had risen like a squashed orange and was climbing the eastern sky.

The witch kept shaking out more soaring powder over them all. They went higher and higher. The wind whistled by. Even the bats could hardly keep up with them.

In spite of the spider's advice, the kittens shut their eyes tight, but they dug their claws into the broom deeper than ever. They were determined to hold on.

Now and again the broom seemed to swerve
perilously, or there was an added rush of sound as
if other objects were passing them. Two and Too
Many dared open their eyes just a slit. Now they
saw that they certainly were in a race! Other
brooms with strange riders were also in the sky.
Some had witches and some had goblins, but all
had black cat-pilots whose eyes blazed bright as
headlights.

The kittens were amazed. They stared. Their
eyes opened wider and wider with astonishment.
Now their broom was close to overtaking another.

Suddenly there was a scream from the rider they
had just passed.

"Tail-lights! Look, she's got tail-lights!"

"Whoever heard of such a thing? It isn't in the
rules!" shrieked another witch.

"It's an innovation," yelled a goblin. "Wish I had
thought of that too!"

"Twin tail-lights! They are dazzling me,"
screamed another rider, wobbling badly.

There was a terrific commotion in the sky.

Riders swerved off course and collided. Brooms got tangled. Cat-pilots lashed their tails and spat at each other.

In the midst of it all, Blackington and the witch and their broom (with the all-unsuspecting tail-lights) shot ahead. Over the moon they went and were FIRST at the goal. There they landed safely, at the PLACE-EXACTLY-BETWEEN-NIGHT-AND-MORNING.

What a reception they were given!

The Great Sky-Witch Queen fastened the cov-
eted Moon Pin on the witch's hat, shook hands, and
congratulated her and Blackington.

"Now," she said, "tell me about your new tail-
lights. They sound like a fine invention."

The witch was speechless. Then Blackington,
rubbing self-consciously against her legs, came
forward.

"Just a little idea I had," he said (which was not, of course, exactly true). He called to Two and Too Many to come forward.

Bravely they walked out of their hiding place in the big besom and sat gazing up at the great Sky-Witch Queen, their eyes wide and shining.

"Boddikins and beeswax," she grinned, "wherever did you find them?"

"Oh, Your Majesty," replied the witch, "I leave all such details to my pilot, Blackington."

The big cat purred grandly, but said no more.

It was five minutes to morning by the time the broom circled its way down into the wood and came to rest in front of the crooked cottage. The witch climbed off stiffly. The kittens hopped off and stretched themselves, then helped Blackington and the witch to carry the broom inside. The spiders throbbed on their webs in welcome. The bats settled back on their beams in the roof.

"Well, Blackington," said the witch proudly, "we made it! But, you know, those tail-lights were what did it. Where are they now? Let me take a good look at them."

She lit the candle and glared down at Two and Too Many who had come out of the shadows at a signal from Blackington and stood side by side in front of the witch.

"Fillikins, billikins," she grinned. Now, ugly as she was, the kittens could clearly see the twinkle in her eye. "Where did they come from?"

Blackington waved his tail meaningfully.

"Why didn't you tell me about them before?"

Blackington spread his front paws in a curious gesture.

"I suppose you thought I'd say it was two too many," chuckled the witch. "Well, they are indispensable now. Mine for keeps. Take good care of them, Blackington. Who knows, we may win again next year! Now scat, all of you. Get busy, for I'm starving!"

With that, she hung up her tall hat and beamed at the new Moon Pin. She dragged off her cloak, kicked off her shoes and, giving a huge yawn, turned to wind the clock.

Blackington and the kittens began to fry frogs'
legs for breakfast.